big fat hen

ILLUSTRATED BY

KEITH BAKER

VOYAGER BOOKS
HARCOURT BRACE & COMPANY
SAN DIEGO   NEW YORK   LONDON

PRINTED IN SINGAPORE

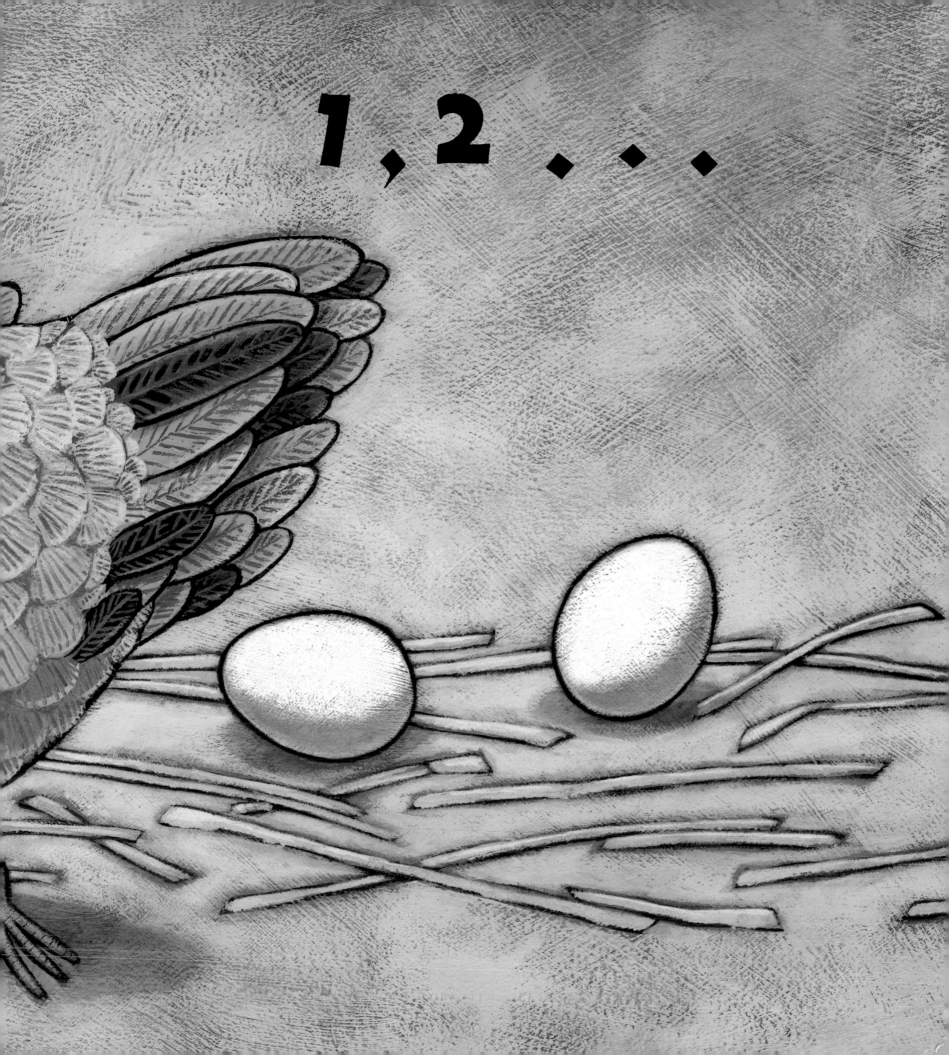

buckle my shoe

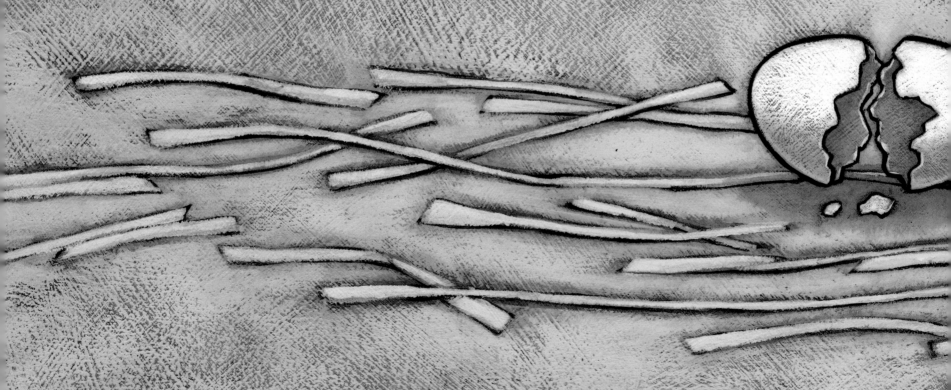

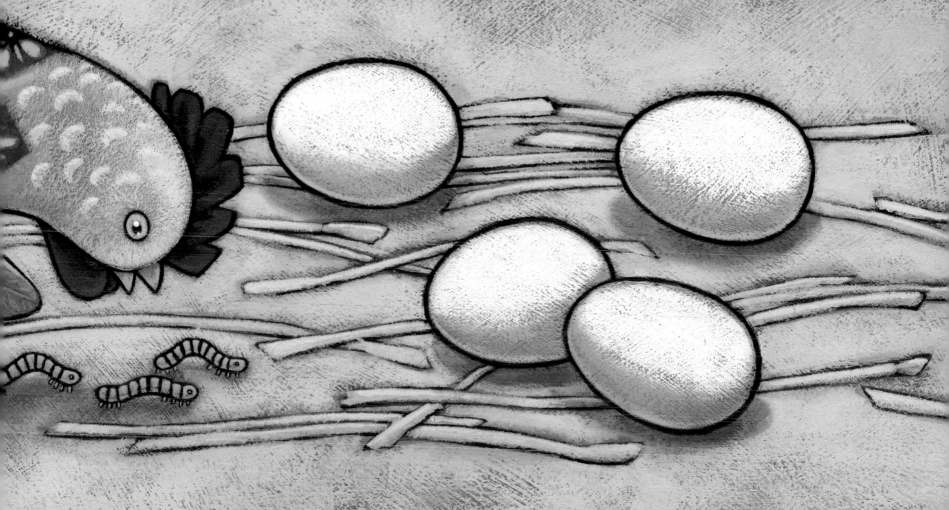

shut the door

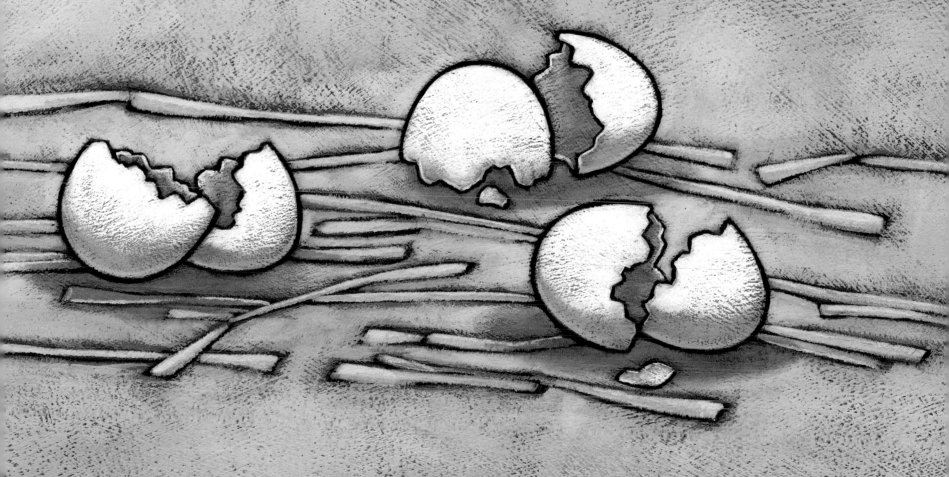

5, 6 . . .

pick up sticks

lay them straight

a big

fat hen

and

her friends

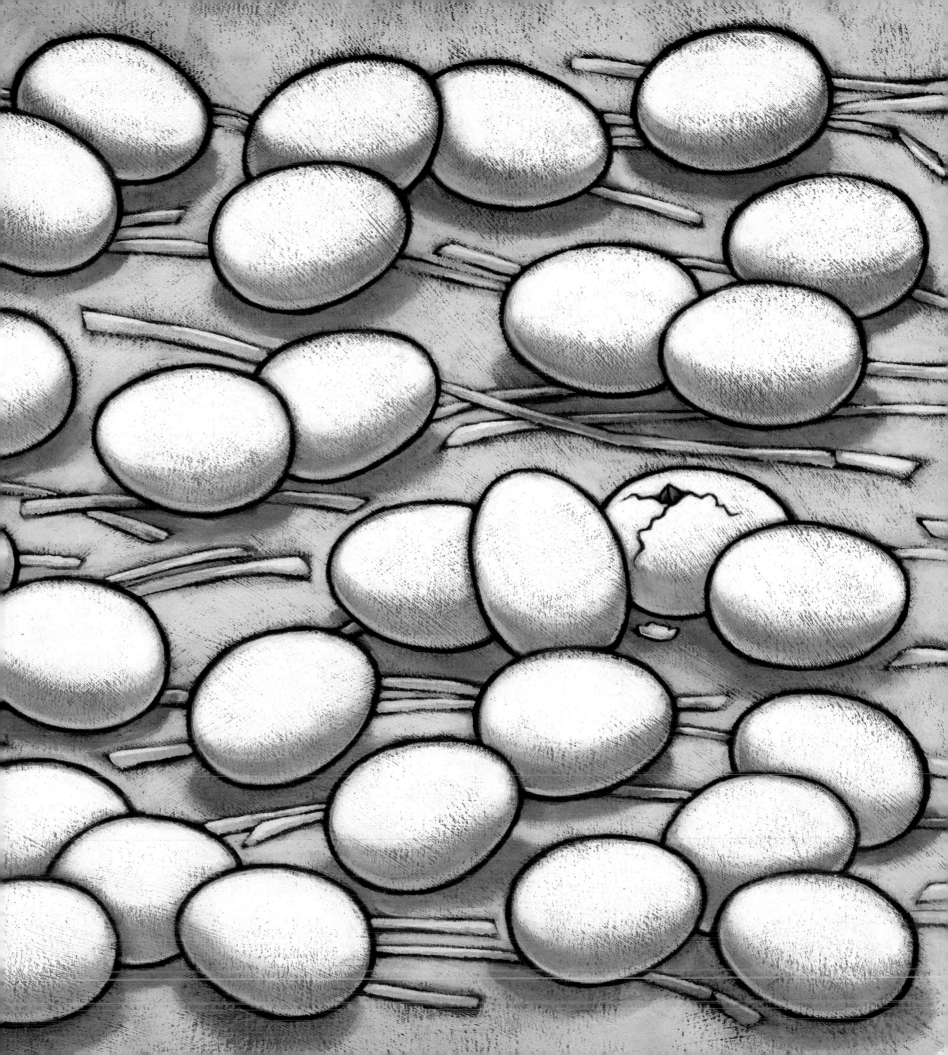

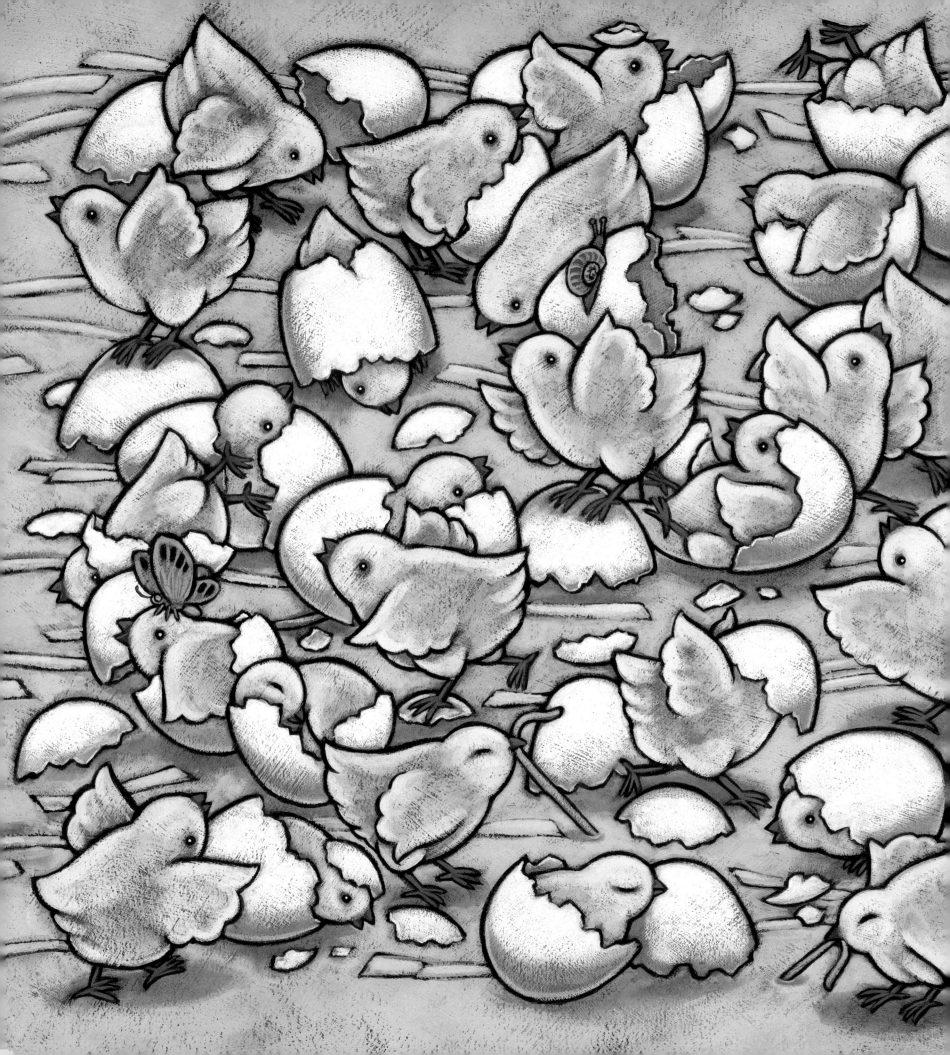

and all
their chicks!

First Voyager Books edition 1999
Voyager Books is a registered trademark of Harcourt Brace & Company.

The Library of Congress has cataloged the hardcover edition as follows:
Baker, Keith, 1953–
Big fat hen/Keith Baker.—1st ed.
p.   cm.
Summary: Big Fat Hen counts to ten with her friends
and all their chicks.
ISBN 0-15-292869-3
ISBN 0-15-201951-0 pb
ISBN 0-15-201331-8 board book
1. Nursery rhymes. 2. Children's poetry.
[1. Nursery rhymes. 2. Counting.] I. Title.
PZ8.3.B175Bi 1994
[E]—dc20   93-19160

J I N O M K

The illustrations in this book were done in
Liquitex acrylics on illustration board.
The text and display type were hand-lettered by Georgia Deaver.
Color separations by Bright Arts, Ltd., Singapore
Printed and bound by Tien Wah Press, Singapore
Production supervision by Stanley Redfern and Jane Van Gelder
Designed by Trina Stahl